MR. MEN
LITTLE MISS
Try Again

Roger Hargreaves

Original concept by
Roger Hargreaves

With grateful thanks to
Dr. Elizabeth Kilbey

D0522821

This is a story about resilience.

Mr Bump was always having accidents.

As you may have heard, if there was something for Mr Bump to bump into, he'd bump into it.

BUMP!

But Mr Bump would always get back up and try again, even when he wanted to give up.

Are you able to bounce back when challenges come your way?

This is what being resilient means.

One day, Mr Bump was having a particularly clumsy day.

He tripped over a leaf.

Yes, you heard me right, a leaf.

And he fell flat on the ground.

OUCH!

Then, as Mr Bump was getting up, he accidentally caught his foot in his bandages.

Can you guess what happened next?

That's right, Mr Bump sent himself spinning along the path and bumped into a tree.

BUMP!

Poor Mr Bump.

Even his bandages couldn't hide his blushes.

But do you think Mr Bump gave up and went home?

No, Mr Bump was resilient. He could recover from whatever setbacks came his way.

How do you feel after something difficult has happened?

You may have thought this story was about Mr Bump being resilient.

But what happened next is really what this story is about.

Mr Bump was about to spend some time with Little Miss Brave.

Little Miss Brave is very brave. She is not afraid of heights or spiders or thunderstorms.

She is not afraid of standing up for others or what she believes in.

Are you brave like Little Miss Brave?

I'm sure you are sometimes, but what do you do when things go wrong?

Mr Bump dusted himself off and decided to join Little Miss Brave.

"Would you like to help me at my Extreme Sports Day?" she asked.

"That sounds like lots of fun," smiled Mr Bump.

So, the friends made their way to Little Miss Brave's house.

As you may not know, Little Miss Brave's house is on the edge of a cliff, so it's the perfect place for rock climbing, mountain biking and abseiling.

She had also set up a giant zip-wire and a huge skatepark with elaborate ramps.

Little Miss Somersault wanted to try the mountain biking.

Mr Tickle's long limbs were perfect for rock climbing.

And Mr Cool is a skateboarder extraordinaire, who couldn't wait to show off his tricks at the skatepark!

But not everyone was feeling as brave about the extreme sports.

Little Miss Fun had been excited about the giant zip-wire, but when she saw how long and high it was, she felt very nervous.

"I'm not sure I can do it," she trembled.

And despite Little Miss Brave's encouragement, she saw that many of her friends also stood hesitantly at the top of the cliff.

Little Miss Brave decided that the best thing to do was to show them how much fun the activities were.

"Just think of all the new and scary things you've done before that you've enjoyed," said Little Miss Brave. "You may surprise yourself when you give it a go!"

And with that, Little Miss Brave got on her mountain bike.

But unfortunately, with all eyes on her, Little Miss Brave started to feel worried.

Mountain biking was harder than she remembered, and she wasn't confident she could make it down the cliff.

Despite what she had said, Little Miss Brave was scared.

"You're almost there, Little Miss Brave!" cheered Mr Bump, encouragingly.

Though it didn't feel like that to Little Miss Brave, as her fingers gripped the handlebars and her bike wobbled on the rocks.

A very relieved Little Miss Brave reached the bottom of the cliff, but sadly, her wobbly ride hadn't persuaded everyone else to have a go.

Little Miss Brave was worried that her Extreme Sports Day would be a disaster.

"Why don't I climb the rocks alongside you, Mr Tickle?" she offered.

"Yes, please!" said Mr Tickle. "It would be great if you can show me what to do."

But Mr Tickle actually turned out to be a natural rock climber, while Little Miss Brave found it difficult and really felt like giving up.

"You can do it!" shouted Mr Bump, as Little Miss Brave struggled to regain her hold on the rocks. "You just need to try again and have confidence that it will go right this time."

And do you know what?

Her persistence paid off.

Little Miss Brave reached the top of the cliff, feeling proud of herself for keeping going when she'd felt so disheartened.

Now the Extreme Sports Day was properly underway! Little Miss Brave was pleased and relieved. She decided it was time to celebrate by going down the giant zip-wire, but unfortunately, she didn't propel herself properly and ended up hanging in mid-air.

Do you know what Mr Bump did?

He took to the zip-wire and they glided down together!

"Thank you, Mr Bump!" smiled Little Miss Brave. "I thought I was the one who'd be helping you. But you've taught me that sometimes it's not about being brave enough to try things, but about being resilient and bouncing back when things go wrong."

Which is exactly what was about to happen as Mr Bump reached the end of the zip-wire.

BUMP!